The Factory Frogs of Figgle Nooch

Tracy Rae Hart

Illustrated by M. Isnaenie

Publisher's Information

EBookBakery Books

Author contact: editingwithhart@gmail.com

ISBN 978-1-953080-42-4

Author Tracy Rae Hart
with illustrations by M. Isnaenie

Dedication

This book was always for Daniel...

And is also dedicated to Mom
who has been eager to see it go into the world,

Thank you to: my brother, Michael, for the original illustration ideas,
feedback from my CCW writing group: Maggie Hayes, Becky Demetrick,
Rebecca Maizel, Linda Melino, Ashley Bray and
Mariellen Langworthy; and Patrice Newman.
And deep gratitude for
I. Michael Grossman for prodding me and producing this book!

A cheerful boy with a friendly pooch
resides in the town of Figgle Nooch.
He lives with his uncle, Johnny Von Hatcher,
a grouchy man, the official frog catcher.

This autumn day, breezes blow cool.

Daniel zig-zags home after school.

Sees his uncle wiggling his knees,

scratching his body like a pup whose got fleas.

"Daniel," he croaks, "you must learn my trade.
I'm too itchy to work, but need to get paid.
Frogging is serious, stress is intense.
We'll walk to the swamp, out back, past the fence."

They trudge by the orchard and reach Biggle's Bog.

"Now, Dan," says his uncle, "look sharp for a frog.

We'll catch it

PA-SWOOP!

with my thick, sturdy net.

The trick's to stay dry; try not to forget!"

Dan looks to the left, sweeps eyes to the right.

For nearly an hour, no jumpers in sight.

But across wavy water, what does he spy?

A glistening frog springing up to the sky!

SPRONGO!

The frog leaps high with joy.

Daniel giggles. "It's a living toy!

We can jump together. We'll swim. We'll play!

I'll build him a house with sticks and damp clay."

But right in front of poor Daniel's eyes,

PA-SWOOP!

Uncle's net traps the frog by surprise!

Scratching, he whispers, "Quick, follow me.
We'll take it downtown to the frog factory."

Daniel's mouth opens, but what can he say?

Uncle's old views are not easy to sway.

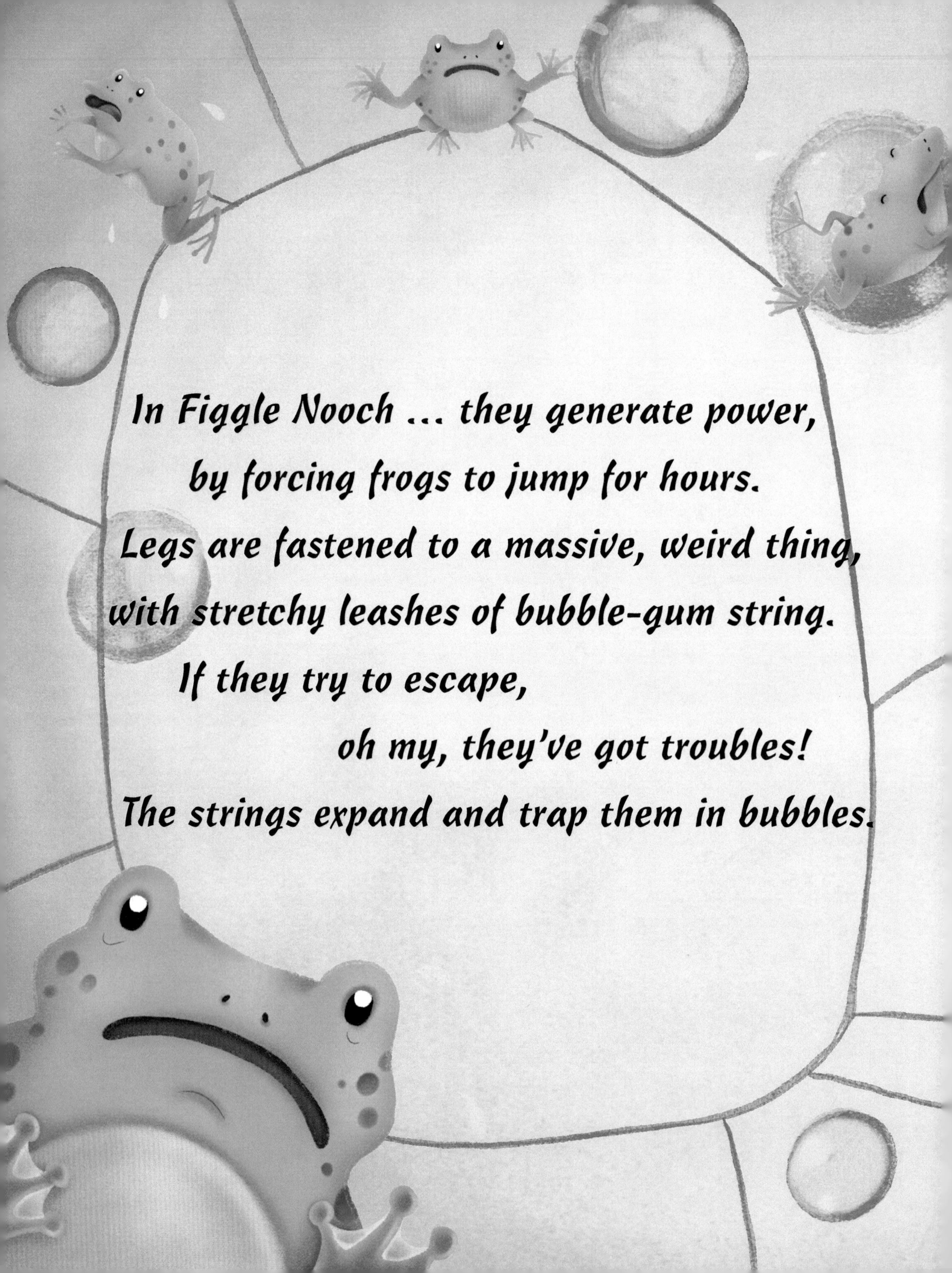

In Figgle Nooch ... they generate power,

by forcing frogs to jump for hours.

Legs are fastened to a massive, weird thing,

with stretchy leashes of bubble-gum string.

If they try to escape,

oh my, they've got troubles!

The strings expand and trap them in bubbles.

Frogs don't get vacations. Frogs don't get a break.
And when it's their birthday, they don't get a cake.
No cake on their birthday! Does that make you sad?
Well in Figgle Nooch Village, the frogs have it bad.

Clang! Whizo! Poppers! Mizzoola, Ker-flooey!
screeches the gizmo that squirts gum so gooey.

"Lamps in the village that click dark to bright
glow because croakers jump all through the night?
These frogs look so thin. They seem awful shy.
These frogs are unhappy." Dan starts to cry.
There's no joyful leaping.
And, oh, worse than that!
His uncle is dropping HIS frog in the vat.

Uncle lies down (his bumps raw and red).
Dan knows he needs to start using his head.

'I'll free them,' he thinks, 'destroy that machine...
Find a solution that's clever and clean.
I'll plan and I'll plot to discover a way
for the frogs to return to their water ballet.

Perhaps a brisk hike
will jolt my brain's juice,
spark an idea
I can put to good use.'

Where is his dog? He had been at his heel.
Here he comes now – in his mouth – a pinwheel?
It spins in a circle. It whirls round with ease,
spurred on by the surge of a blustery breeze.

"That's it!" Daniel whoops, racing back down the hill.

"The answer's so simple: we'll build a windmill!"

At the Town Meeting, Dan raises his hand.
"Frogs live in water. Why are they on land?
But I know a new way to power our town."

The people guffaw, and a few even frown.
"Hey, kid, sit your bum down on one of those stools.
Life's fine as it is, with old habits and rules."

Daniel thinks, 'But it's not fair.'
Pictures the frogs, and yells, "Wait! I care!
I have something important to say!
Windmills are better than frogs any day."

The Figgle Nooch crowd is surprised, frankly stunned.
Why, this topnotch idea feels like a home run!

One woman speaks up.
"Why should we be annoyed?
If we build windmills, we'll all be employed.
Besides, as you know, frogs are harder to find.
But here, wind is constant,
come rain or come shine."

Daniel's a champion. He shouts, "Yip! Yippee!
Frogs don't have to work. They are free!
They are free!"

Several months later, the windmills stand tall,
producing their voltage from breezes or squall.
It's time to release them. Dan opens the door,
cuts sticky leashes; frogs scoot to the floor.
They gaze at their hero and if able to speak,
would have heartily thanked him, if not feeling weak.

The way that he leads them outside is quite wise:
townsfolk had filled fifteen jars full of flies.
They buzz off on gusts,
blowing down towards the glade.
The frogs croak in song as they form a parade!

And in Figgle Nooch Village to this very day,

they use wind for power and let the frogs play.

Made in United States
North Haven, CT
26 November 2023